GIRLS SURVIVE

Published by Stone Arch Books, an imprint of Capstone
1710 Roe Crest Drive,
North Mankato, Minnesota 56003
capstonepub.com

Library of Congress Cataloging-in-Publication Data is available on the
Library of Congress website.
ISBN: 9781663990556 (hardcover)
ISBN: 9781666330625 (paperback)
ISBN: 9781666330632 (ebook PDF)

Summary: Twelve-year-old Audrey wants nothing more than to be a dance
performer and aerialist, but that feels far from reality in 1944 Hartford,
Connecticut. So when she learns the Ringling Bros. and Barnum & Bailey
Circus is coming to town, Audrey is determined to be there under the big top.
It's her only chance to see the Flying Wallendas, a world-renowned high-wire
act, perform. Audrey convinces her mother to let her take her six-year-old twin
sisters with her to the show. But disaster strikes when a fire breaks out under
the big top. Can Audrey escape—and find her siblings—before the tent comes
crashing down?

Editorial Credits
Editor: Alison Deering; Designer: Kay Fraser;
Production Specialist: Katy LaVigne

Image Credits: Shutterstock: demonique (geometric background),
Max Lashcheuski (background texture)

AUDREY
UNDER
THE BIG TOP

A Hartford Circus Fire Survival Story

by Jessica Gunderson

illustrated by Wendy Tan

STONE ARCH BOOKS
a capstone imprint

CHAPTER ONE

I hoped I could catch her this time. Charlotte took a step forward. Her bottom lip twitched in fear. Our eyes met, and I gave her an encouraging smile, but I wasn't sure she trusted me. Not after last time.

Behind me the crowd rustled. Someone yawned. A song blared from the record player.

I tuned out the sounds and focused my thoughts on my little sister. I smiled at Charlotte again. She was nearing the end of the fence now. Her balancing act was nearly over. All she had to do was a final twirl, then jump into my waiting arms.

Last time we'd done this routine, I hadn't been able to catch her. I'd tried, but we'd both tumbled under Charlotte's weight. We hadn't been hurt, but the fall had made Charlotte's fear of heights much worse.

Looking at my sister's face, I should have realized that she wasn't going to do the twirl this time. Instead, Charlotte jumped, several seconds too soon.

In the split second she was suspended in air, I rushed forward. Charlotte landed perfectly in my arms. The crowd cheered.

I set my sister on her feet. "Give a round of applause for Charlotte, one of the Amazing Adams Twins!"

Charlotte bowed quickly, then ran to her twin's side. Charlotte didn't like the attention, but Patty was the opposite—she waved to the crowd and smiled.

"Ladies and gentlemen," Patty called in her high-pitched, six-year-old voice, "I present Audrey the Acrobat!"

I smirked at the words ladies and gentlemen. The crowd was mostly just neighborhood kids, gathered to watch my sisters and me—Audrey the Acrobat and the Amazing Adams Twins—perform. All the usual kids were here—the Walker girls, the Jimenez kids, the Tucker crew.

But today the audience wasn't just little kids. This time, Will Murphy, a boy in my class at school, was here too.

I avoided looking toward Will. I couldn't be nervous now. It was time for the finale. I moved toward the huge oak tree, snapping my fingers at Charlotte. It was her cue to put a new record on the player.

When I heard the first notes coming through the open window, I shimmied up the tree to the lowest branch. I stood on the branch, waving my arms to the beat of the song. As the beat picked up, I climbed higher and higher.

If I fell from this height, I could die. Or worse, I could break my leg and never perform again.

I was only twelve years old, but I already knew what I wanted. I wanted to be a performer someday. If I fell now, I might never perform on a trapeze in front of thousands of people. I might never join the Ringling Bros. and Barnum & Bailey Circus.

I sidled along one of the top branches, the strongest and thickest one that I knew could hold me. Then I closed my eyes.

I couldn't see anything in front of me. I took one cautious step, then another. A hot wind brushed my face.

"Open your eyes or you'll fall!" shrieked a child's voice below me.

"*Shhh*," hissed another voice. "It's all part of the act!"

I tried hard to keep a straight face and not break my concentration. I pushed one toe forward along the tree branch. It wobbled a bit, but I knew it would hold me. I had practiced this act countless times before. I couldn't wait to tell my dad I had finally done it in front of an audience.

If I could pull off the ending, that was.

I missed my dad. More than three years ago, after Japanese soldiers had bombed American ships in Pearl Harbor, the United States entered the Second World War. My dad had enlisted right away.

Now he was off at war, serving as a medic for the U.S. Army in Italy. He'd only been able to come home a handful of times since he'd left. My little sisters barely remembered him.

Last month, the Allied forces had scored a victory when our troops stormed the beaches of Normandy, France. On the radio, reporters said Paris might soon be freed from German occupation.

Maybe that means the war will be over soon and Dad can come home, I'd thought as I listened. *Then he can watch my performances and cheer me on like he used to.*

Dad had always supported my dream to be a famous aerialist. My mother, on the other hand, always told me to be realistic.

"We're just an ordinary family in Connecticut," she would say.

I knew Mom was tired from working all the time to make ends meet. Anything extra, she saved for college for me, Patty, and Charlotte.

I didn't understand why I needed to go to college if I wanted to be a performer. I would have rather had the money for dance lessons and gymnastics.

All summer, I'd been helping take care of Patty and Charlotte while Mom was at work. And three weeks ago, Mom had given me something special as a thank you—tickets to the Ringling Bros. and Barnum & Bailey Circus. I couldn't wait, especially for the aerial act, the Flying Wallendas.

I'd been counting down the days. And now, only two days left.

I peeked at the crowd through my eyelashes and immediately wished I hadn't. Vivian Lang—my number-one rival—had joined the crowd. She was standing next to Will, arms crossed, a smug look on her pretty face.

Vivian wanted to be a performer too. She always got the lead role in all the school plays. And her family could afford all the dance and gymnastics lessons she wanted.

Now that Vivian is here, I definitely have to pull off my trick, I told myself.

The wind blew again, rustling my hair. The tree branch swayed beneath my feet, and I wobbled, circling my arms to regain my balance.

The kids below hushed. Silence was all around me. The branch swayed again, and my mouth dropped into a surprised O.

Then I fell.

CHAPTER TWO

For a moment, I was suspended in air.

The silence turned to screams and gasps.

But I wasn't worried. This was all part of the act. I knew exactly when my fingers would grasp the branch below.

When my hands gripped the branch, I opened my eyes in mock surprise. My legs dangled wildly.

The kids' shrieks descended into silence again. I heard one giggle, then another. Then they all broke into laughter.

But I wasn't done. I pumped my legs, swinging back and forth. Then I let go.

I flipped my body in midair, hooking my legs around a lower branch. I kept the momentum going, swinging upside down, going back and forth once, twice, three times.

Then I flipped off the branch and did a somersault in midair. I landed on my feet in front of the crowd, just as the song on the record player ended.

Everyone clapped. I bowed and grinned. A yellow daisy landed at my feet.

I blushed, hoping Will was the one who had plucked it and thrown it. I picked it up and snuck a glance at him.

Vivian was still standing next to him. She tapped her foot as though impatient and bored. But I could tell that, despite her demeanor, she was impressed.

"Thank you! Thank you!" I cried, taking another bow.

Even though our spectators today were just little kids, I still relished the applause. I couldn't wait until I could perform in front of a real audience.

"I couldn't do it without the Amazing Adams Twins," I said, motioning for Charlotte and Patty to stand next to me.

The twins shuffled forward. Patty smiled and gave a bow. Charlotte, however, stared at the ground, twisting her toe in the grass.

I frowned. I knew Charlotte didn't like being the center of attention, but if we ever wanted to be as famous as the Flying Wallendas—the most famous family of aerialists in the world—she would have to get used to it.

Someday we would be just like them—Audrey the Acrobat and the Amazing Adams Twins.

I grabbed Patty's waist and lifted her high into the air. Then I twirled us both around.

"Let's hear it for Patty!" I said as the crowd cheered.

When the applause stopped, I set her down and reached for Charlotte.

Charlotte stiffened. She didn't like when I lifted her up. She liked her feet on the ground at all times.

But we had to give the audience what they wanted. I twirled with her as the crowd clapped a final time.

The applause died away, and I set Charlotte down. She and Patty linked arms with the Walker girls and skipped across the lawn.

I tucked the daisy I hoped Will had thrown behind my ear. He was still standing next to Vivian. When he saw me looking, he waved me over.

"Brilliant performance," he said in a formal accent. "Quite splendid."

Vivian smiled, but it looked a little forced. "I only saw the last bit," she said. "I bet my gymnastics teacher could help you stick the landing better, though."

The hair on the back of my neck stood up. "I don't need coaching—" I began.

A screen door slammed. "Audrey!" my mother called from the back steps. "Girls! Come inside. A letter from your father has arrived!"

Vivian's smug smile drooped a little. Her father had been killed early on in the war. But if anyone at school brought it up, she insisted it didn't bother her. "I barely remember him," she would say.

I doubted it was true.

"You better go in," Vivian said. She nudged Will's shoulder. "Walk me home?"

I didn't stick around to hear his response. Instead, I headed for the house, shrugging off Vivian's unpleasant vibes.

I couldn't wait to read my father's letter. He always wrote to each of us girls separately, even though the twins couldn't read yet. Our mother always had to read theirs aloud.

My mother held the letter out to me as I bounded up the back steps.

"How was work?" I asked her. "You just missed our performance!"

Mom mumbled a tired response. She worked as a launderer at a hotel and didn't like her job very much. I knew that's why she wanted to send us girls to college—so we didn't have to work a job like that ourselves.

In my bedroom, I read my father's letter. He told me about Italy, the hot sun, and the beautiful villas.

If we weren't at war, he wrote, *I'd think I was on a vacation.*

He also told me how he had stayed up late helping one of his patients write a love letter to his girl back home. The soldier didn't like his own penmanship, so he had my father rewrite the letter for him.

The lesson is to practice your penmanship, he wrote, *so you can write your own love letters when you are older.*

I laughed. I liked that my father wrote so honestly.

He ended the letter, like he always did, with the words *Be brave*.

I wrote back right away, paying close attention to my penmanship.

As I wrote, I glanced up at the circus posters that hung on my walls. My father had always understood my love of the circus and performing.

I knew he'd love hearing about our performance that afternoon. I knew he would understand.

I would have to be brave to achieve my dream of becoming a performer. My mother might be determined for me to go to college, but I had other plans.

CHAPTER **THREE**

Hartford, Connecticut
Barbour Street
July 5, 1944
1:50 p.m.

"Hurry up!" I called.

The twins were lagging behind, and I had no patience for it. I couldn't wait to get to the circus. I'd hardly slept at all last night. My dreams had been peppered with tightrope walkers, big-band songs, bright lights, and the smell of popcorn.

I couldn't get to the circus grounds fast enough.

"It's hot," complained Patty.

She was right. The sun was bright and the humidity was thick. I could only imagine what it would be like under the big top, with thousands of people crammed inside.

I wished my mother would walk a little faster too. I knew she was tired from work, but still. She seemed to be enjoying herself as we strolled toward the circus grounds.

Patty and Charlotte skipped along beside us, their ribbons bouncing in their hair. They always wore the same ribbons—Charlotte yellow and Patty purple. The ribbons helped others tell them apart, although my mom and I knew at a glance. We didn't need ribbons to tell us.

The twins ran ahead of us, their footsteps matching time. They both launched into a cartwheel at the same time.

It amazed me that my sisters always seemed to know what the other was going to do. They were too young to explain why, but my mom called it their "twin sense."

"I'm glad you took the day off," I told my mom.

She smiled at me. "I know how much you've been looking forward to the circus," she said. "You deserve to have fun. You've been looking after your sisters all summer."

"I hope I see Marjory!" I exclaimed. "And Lucia too!"

Marjory and Lucia were my closest friends from school, but I didn't get to see them often anymore. At the end of the school year, we had promised to try to see each other over the summer. But my responsibilities to my family had taken over.

I led the way up Barbour Street toward the circus grounds. A few cars whizzed past on their way to the grounds, but otherwise the neighborhood seemed quiet—too quiet.

Something is wrong, I thought.

No smells of popcorn and cotton candy wafted through the air. No giggles of children. No shouts from workers at sideshows along the midway, calling for spectators.

When we rounded the corner, my heart plummeted.

There was no big top tent skewering the clouds.

I took off at a run, ignoring the shouts of my mother behind me. I entered the grounds and saw dozens of circus wagons. Horses still stood in their pens. Workers bustled, carrying benches, chairs, and poles.

I looked around, puzzled but relieved. *Did we get the time wrong?*

I glanced down at my ticket. No, the show was supposed to start at two-fifteen, just a few minutes from now.

A grizzled worker, his arms full of wooden boards and tools, paused next to me. "Can I help you, miss?" he asked. Sweat glistened on his brow. The heat today was brutal.

"I am supposed to attend the circus," I told him. "Is it running late?"

The man laughed. "I guess you haven't heard the news," he said. "The afternoon performance was canceled. You won't be going to any circus today."

No performance. I couldn't believe what I was hearing. No circus, no Flying Wallendas. I looked down at my ticket again. The thick tears in my eyes blurred my vision.

"What happened?" I asked.

The man softened his tone when he saw my expression. "Sorry, miss. Trains were late. Been happening a lot lately. War supplies take priority on the rails. Nothing we could do."

I looked at him. My tears had retreated, and instead anger filled me. "You don't understand!"

I said. "I have to see the Flying Wallendas. I just have to!"

The man looked down at my ticket. "Tell you what. Come with me. We'll see if we can exchange this for tomorrow's show instead."

I looked back and saw my mom and sisters lingering on the sidewalk, watching. "Theirs too?" I asked.

The man followed my gaze and nodded. "We'll give it a try."

I ran to my family and told them the news. Then I returned to the man.

"My name's Chuck," he said. "What's yours?"

"Audrey," I told him as we walked toward where the big top was being set up.

Canvas panels lay stretched across the ground. Elephants stood nearby. A worker shouted an order, and the elephants moved forward, pulling on ropes to hoist up the canvas walls.

"Audrey the Acrobat, actually," I said. "My twin sisters and I perform aerial shows all the time. We'll be famous someday, just like the Flying Wallendas!"

As soon as the words were out of my mouth, embarrassment flushed my cheeks. I expected Chuck would laugh at my dreams of fame, but to my surprise, he didn't. He nodded.

"Good to start young," he said. "I never had those kinds of dreams. I like the backstage life. Been doing it most of my life."

"Do you know the Flying Wallendas?" I asked. "I mean, personally?"

This time he did laugh. "Sure do. They're good folks. Hard workers, like most of us in the circus world."

Chuck led me to the ticket station. I showed the agent our tickets, and he exchanged them for four new tickets for the next day's afternoon performance. Chuck waved goodbye as I skipped back toward my mom and sisters.

The twins squealed when I showed them the new tickets. But Mom shook her head sadly. "Audrey, I can't take another day off to go to the circus."

"Can't we just go by ourselves?" I asked. "I'm twelve now. Practically an adult!"

Mom was silent for a moment, thinking. "Thousands of people will be here," she said. "You can't let the twins out of your sight."

"I'll keep a close eye on them," I said. "I swear!"

Mom frowned, thinking.

"It's a circus," I reminded her. "What could go wrong at a circus?"

Finally, Mom gave a slow nod. "Okay," she said. "Just be careful."

I smiled at her. "They'll be safe with me. I promise."

"Look at her!" Patty cried.

She pointed at a hippopotamus rolling in a tank of water. We were wandering through the animal menagerie tent on our way to the big top.

I inched the girls through the crowd to get a closer look. "It's Betty Lou!" I said. Betty Lou was a pygmy hippo. She had survived a circus fire two years earlier in Cleveland. No people had been hurt when the menagerie tent went up in flames, but forty-five animals had died. Betty Lou was a survivor.

"She is magnificent!" Charlotte exclaimed.

I smiled at her, happy she was using one of the big words I'd taught her.

We moved through the tent. Giraffes craned their long necks. Elephants wiggled their trunks

in the air. A kangaroo hopped up and down in its cage.

Patty hopped up and down, in time with the kangaroo. "Can we get one as a pet?" she asked.

"Can you . . . imagine a kangaroo . . . ," I sang. "A kangaroo . . . for you!"

The twins giggled, and a few other kids near us laughed too. I loved having an audience.

My sisters and I left the animal tent and strolled down the midway. At the end of the midway, the big top stretched tall and wide, longer than a football field.

The tent was so big it could hold thousands of people. The white canvas roof sloped upward, held in place by tent poles. The poles, topped with American flags, speared the sky, waving in the breeze.

The midway was lined with sideshow booths. We stopped to watch a sword-swallower. Inch by inch, the man pushed the sword down his throat. The twins were silent as they watched him, their eyes wide.

I led the girls to the next sideshow. This one was my favorite. A trapeze artist swung from bar to bar, flipping and twisting in midair. Her sequined costume glittered as it caught the sun.

She landed and curtsied. The small crowd applauded. My claps were the loudest. The crowd drifted away, but I waited.

The artist ducked out the side of the small tent and sat down on an overturned pail. I watched as she fanned herself with a folded piece of paper.

I took a step toward the performer. "Hello," I said. "That was a great show! How many times did you practice? Have you been in the circus for a long time?"

She looked up at me and shook her head. She no longer wore the smile she'd put on during the show.

I had the feeling she was annoyed, but I wanted her to know how much I admired her.

"I loved how you soared from bar to bar," I said. "It's like you have wings! I want to be just like you someday. I'm Audrey the Acrobat."

The performer shook her head again and stood up. "It's nice to meet you, Audrey," she said. "But let me give you some advice. Go home. You shouldn't be here today."

I stared at her. "What do you mean?"

"You know yesterday's show was canceled?"

I nodded.

"Canceled shows are bad luck," she said. "I'm warning you. Something bad is going to happen."

I took a step backward. Despite the heat, her words chilled me.

"Go on now, Audrey. Go home," the trapeze artist said. Her feather headband shivered in the air as she strode away.

I turned toward the twins, shaking off the foreboding. Nothing was going to stop me from seeing the circus today. Especially not some silly circus superstition.

CHAPTER FOUR

The big top loomed tall and inviting ahead of us. I gave our tickets to the ticket taker, and my sisters and I stepped inside the tent.

Inside, it was dark and cool compared to the hot, sunny grounds. I blinked, letting my eyes adjust.

"Audrey!" a familiar voice shouted.

I looked over to see my friends, Marjory and Lucia. They waved down at us from the highest bleacher in the general admission section.

"Sit with us!" called Lucia.

Still gripping the twins' hands, I started to move toward them. But Charlotte tugged on my hand.

"I don't want to sit up there," she said. "It's too high!"

"But . . . ," I began.

Disappointment wedged in my chest. I hadn't seen my friends all summer. And the top row had the best view.

Patty tugged on my other hand. "Look!" she said. "It's the Walkers!"

She wriggled out of my grip and ran toward our neighbors. Charlotte and I followed after her more slowly.

"Hello, Audrey," Mrs. Walker said. "Is your mother here too?"

I shook my head. "We were supposed to come yesterday, but the show was canceled," I explained. "Mom couldn't take two days off work."

"Audrey is mad," Charlotte broke in. "She wants to sit with her friends. Way, way, way up there." She pointed to the bleachers. "But I'm too scared."

I gave Charlotte a hug. "It's okay," I told her.

"The twins can sit with us," Mrs. Walker offered. "We're across the tent in the southeast bleachers."

"Yes! Yes!" the Walker girls shouted, jumping up and down in excitement.

I hesitated, remembering my promise to my mother. I wouldn't let the twins out of my sight.

But, I reasoned, *I'll be leaving them in good hands with Mrs. Walker. I know exactly where they'll be, and I'll be sitting just across the big top. What's the worst that could happen?*

"Thank you," I told Mrs. Walker. "I'll be back for them right after the show."

I turned and smiled excitedly at my friends. Then I bid the twins goodbye. As they waved at me, I stopped cold. Echoing in my head was the performer's warning: *Something bad is going to happen.*

I swallowed and shook off the feeling. *It's just a superstition*, I told myself. *Nothing is going to happen.*

I looked up at the high wires and trapezes that crisscrossed the tent. Excitement overtook the doom. I couldn't wait to see the Flying Wallendas!

I bounded up the bleachers to Marjory and Lucia. Lucia was in the middle of telling about her family's new purchase—a telephone.

"I'll give you my phone number," she said.

"We don't have a telephone," I said.

"Neither do we," Marjory added.

"You'll have to get one!" Lucia exclaimed. "We can talk to each other, even though we're blocks away!"

"But doesn't it take a long time for your words to travel through all those wires?" Marjory asked. "I've never figured out how that works."

A singsong voice broke in near me. "We have a telephone."

I groaned inside. Vivian.

Sure enough, Vivian brushed past me and stood on a lower bleacher, facing us. "But never mind that," she continued. "Look what I have!" She held up a rolled piece of paper.

"Well, what is it?" Marjory asked after a moment.

Vivian smiled widely and shook her long curls. Then she unrolled the paper slowly, pausing for dramatic effect. It was a circus poster. But when I leaned closer, I saw something else—signatures scribbled on the sides.

I gasped. "You got the Flying Wallendas' autographs?"

Vivian nodded. "Yes! My mom arranged for me to meet them. Isn't that swell?"

I swallowed the bubble of jealousy that rose in my throat. "What were they like?" I finally managed.

"Oh, they were absolutely wonderful! They showed me around their dressing wagon," Vivian bragged. "Costumes galore!"

Suddenly I wished I'd sat somewhere else with my sisters instead.

"Shhh!" Lucia hissed at us. "The show is about to start!"

Vivian sat down next to me. The ringmaster stepped into the center ring. "Ladies and gentlemen, boys and girls . . . ," he began.

My heart pounded and my throat felt dry. I should have been enjoying the show, but I couldn't stop looking at the poster in Vivian's hands. Angry sweat trickled down my neck.

"I'm going to get a lemonade," I muttered. "This is just the animal act anyway."

"That's the best one!" Marjory said.

But I was already making my way down the bleachers, sidestepping parents and children as I went.

Main Entrance of the Big Top
July 6, 1944
2:38 p.m.

The lemonade cooled my throat. From the ground next to the bleachers, I watched as animals were paraded into the rings.

Pumas, leopards, and panthers prowled in one ring around their trainer, May Kovar. Polar bears and lions danced in the other two rings.

"Magnificent, isn't it?" a voice from behind me asked.

I turned to see Will Murphy. I blushed a little at the surprise of seeing him.

"I didn't know you were coming to the circus!" I said.

"Well, I'm not a spectator," he said with a smile. "I'm working here! Ringling Bros. often hires local boys to help set up."

I felt a sting of jealousy for the second time today. "Lucky," I said.

He held out his palms to show me his blisters. "My hands don't feel so lucky," he joked.

Loud applause broke out. I looked back at the circus. May Kovar was beginning to lead her big cats out of the ring. The Flying Wallendas were coming on next.

"I'd better get back to my seat," I told Will.

"Bye!" he called after me as I rushed toward the bleachers.

Halfway up the aisle of the bleachers, I stopped to look up. The Wallendas were taking their places on the high wire.

I glanced back at Will to give another wave, but he wasn't looking at me. He had turned around and was staring toward the men's restroom.

I followed his gaze. What I saw made my heart lurch.

A small flame was creeping up the side of the tent. The big top was on fire.

CHAPTER FIVE

I leaped up the remaining bleachers to reach my friends. "Do you see that?" I gasped, pointing at the small fire to the right of us. The flame was no bigger than a fist.

Marjory glanced over and shrugged. "I'm sure someone will put it out." She gestured at the trapezes and high wire. "The Wallendas aren't worried."

Four Wallendas were suspended high above the center ring. A spotlight illuminated their glittery costumes.

It was enough to distract me from the fire. This was the moment I'd been dreaming of.

The Wallendas carried three long balancing poles and a bicycle with no handlebars. On the opposite platform, the leader, Karl Wallenda, clutched a similar bicycle.

Just then, the band broke into a waltz. The Wallendas were about to begin.

I sat, entranced. Herman and Karl Wallenda placed the front wheels of their bicycles on the high wire.

"Look! They're putting the fire out," Lucia said.

I didn't want to turn away from the Wallendas, but I looked over. An usher was lugging a huge bucket toward the fire. Water splashed over the sides. He chucked the water with all his might at the flame.

But the flame flickered on, licking slowly up the side of the tent.

Another usher launched two buckets of water at the flame. A third threw another. But the flame had crawled too high, above the ushers' reach.

"How will they put out the fire now?" Marjory cried.

"I'm sure they will bring out the fire extinguishers," Vivian said. "I saw one when I was meeting the Wallendas."

I heard what my friends were saying, but my attention was on the performers on the high wire. Karl Wallenda had paused on his bicycle. He motioned downward just as Henrietta Wallenda pointed. They'd spotted the flame.

A moment later, the band stopped playing the waltz and launched into "The Stars and Stripes Forever."

My heart fell. The disaster march. I knew from all my reading about the circus that the song was a signal. Something was wrong.

"We have to go!" I said to Marjory.

I tugged on Lúcia's arm. Then I reached for Vivian.

"I came to see the circus," Vivian said firmly. "And I *will* see the circus."

I sat back down. Maybe Vivian was right. We had come to see the circus.

Someone will put out the fire, I told myself.

But the flame was moving quickly along the tent wall, closer and closer to us. Smoke swirled through the air. I coughed.

Next to us, a baby cried. The family stood and walked quickly down the bleachers. Another family followed, the mother waving away smoke with one hand and clutching her child with the other.

The ringmaster ran to the center ring, the long tails of his waistcoat flapping behind him. His top hat bobbed on his head.

"Please stay calm!" he said into the microphone. "Stay in your seats. We will take care of this."

Heat seared across my back. The flames were behind us now.

I swiveled to look, and a bright flash hit my eyes, like someone lighting a giant match. The flames whooshed up the tent wall and onto the ceiling, racing for the pole above us—the pole that held up the west side of the big top.

All around, people were scrambling to get out. One woman fell, rolling down the bleachers and knocking people over like dominoes.

This time, Lucia grabbed my arm. "Let's go!" she cried.

I didn't move. I felt like I was in a trance. I looked to my left and saw that Vivian was gone. So was Marjory.

At the bottom of the bleachers, people had fallen and piled on top of each other. Some were struggling to stand. Others tried to crawl their way out from the bottom of the pile. The bleacher stairs were crammed with frantic people trying to make their way down.

I looked around. People in our section, the one closest to the fire, seemed to be the only ones leaving. My sisters must still be in their seats across the tent.

"The ringmaster told us to stay in our seats," I told Lucia in a soft, determined tone. "I'm staying. Surely someone will put out the fire."

She shook her head in disbelief. Then she made her way down the bleacher seats. At the bottom, she leaped over the mound of people and disappeared.

I sat still, even though sweat dripped down my back and my hair felt as if it was aflame.

Soon, I thought, *the fire will be out and the show will go on.* I would just wait.

Suddenly, though, I realized I was all alone. Everyone had left our section. The heat from the flames at my back was unbearable. I knew I had to get out. But I couldn't leave the tent. Not without the twins.

CHAPTER **SIX**

Inside the Big Top
July 6, 1944
2:42 p.m.

I took the bleachers two at a time and pushed
through the crowd at the bottom.

I didn't know how I would get to the southeast
bleachers. They were on the opposite side of the
big top. If I wasn't careful, I would be carried
along with the crowd, which was heading toward
the nearest exit.

The ringmaster was still begging for calm.
"Please exit in an orderly fashion!" he called.

I rushed past the south grandstands, heading
for the other side of the tent.

Around me, some people were still sitting calmly, waiting for the fire to be put out. Others stood up quickly, knocking over their chairs. One chair toppled down the risers and knocked a woman in the back of the head.

The railings that kept people off the circus arena now penned us in. The movement slowed, and I was trapped in the mass of people.

Someone's elbow dug into my back. Another arm slapped me in the face. People were pushing, trying to barrel forward.

Another whoosh of heat. The fire was growing now, the heat making me light-headed. I thought I might faint.

Someone behind me screamed. Children wailed. As the fire ripped along the seams of the tent, pieces fell like ash from above.

"Charlotte!" I screamed desperately for my sisters. "Patty!"

But it was in vain. My voice only added to the roar of names being called.

I barreled through, shoving and pushing against the flow of people.

"That way, miss!" a man coming toward me yelled. He grabbed my shoulder and tried to spin me around.

"Nooo!" I screamed in his face.

Taken aback, the man let go of my shoulder. I stumbled away, my face streaming with sweat and tears.

A nagging voice inside my head refused to be quiet. *What if the twins are already outside?* it asked. *What if you die trying to save them?*

I silenced the voice. I would keep going. I had to reach the southeast bleachers. I had to know for sure.

Then I spotted a flash of color—one yellow ribbon, one purple. Two identical girls huddled together on grandstand chairs. Their horror-struck eyes watched the crowd moving past them.

The twins. They were alive.

This time, when I yelled their names, the sound echoed toward my sisters' ears. They saw me and burst into tears.

I weaved toward them and grabbed them into a hug. I didn't know how they'd ended up in the grandstands and not in the general admission bleachers.

"Where's Mrs. Walker?" I demanded, looking back and forth from one twin to the other.

The girls didn't answer. They were scared silent.

I tugged my sisters down the risers. It was unbearably hot. I tried to take a deep breath but only inhaled smoke and heat.

Panic had gripped the crowd by now. Some people pushed, others yelled. A little girl lay crying as the crowd stepped over her, streaming toward the exits.

I worried the same thing might happen to the twins if we entered the tangle of panicked people. They could get trampled.

There has to be a better way out, I thought.

I swallowed thickly and realized how frightened I was. I had always thought of myself as brave. My dad always called me that in his letters. But climbing high and performing daring tricks required a different kind of courage. I needed to be brave in a different way.

Still, the thought of climbing made me pause. The fire had ignited the walls and roof on the west side of the tent. But it hadn't reached the sidewall behind the grandstands—not yet.

Maybe we can avoid the frantic crowd, I thought. *We could jump from the top of the grandstands and slip out under the sidewall.*

But we didn't have much time. The sidewall would soon be aflame.

Still clasping the twins' hands, I turned us around. I tugged them up the risers. Empty soda bottles, popcorn, and peanut shells littered the stands. Up and up we went.

The girls were wordless on the climb, gripping my hands tightly. Even Charlotte, who usually protested heights, didn't make a sound. Fear radiated from their silence.

When we reached the top, I let go of the girls' hands.

"Okay, are you ready?" I asked, staring into their wide-eyed faces. They had never looked so alike, identical in their terror. "You're going to do what I tell you."

I saw the fear in Charlotte's eyes as she looked at me, then down at the ground. I looked down too. It was more than a ten-foot drop.

A wave of nervousness flashed over me. But I knew I could do it. I had to. And I'd catch the girls when they jumped, just like we'd practiced so many times.

I turned back to the girls. "I'm going to jump down. Then I'll catch you," I said.

Above, I saw the fire slinking hungrily toward the center of the tent. If the fire latched on to the wooden center pole, it would go up in flames. The big top would collapse. We had to hurry.

I latched my hands around the top riser and swung my legs over the side. Then I let go, dropping easily to the ground.

Twin faces stared down at me. I tried to smile. But what I saw filled me with horror.

The flames were directly above their heads now.

I raised my arms. "One by one," I said. "Just like we're performing at home. Okay?"

I'd barely finished speaking when Patty launched herself into the air, arms flailing as she fell. Her body slammed into mine, and we both fell backward.

For a moment, everything went black. My breath was knocked out of me. Patty rolled off me, and I scrambled to my feet, ready to catch Charlotte.

But no one was standing on the top riser. Charlotte was gone.

CHAPTER **SEVEN**

"Charlotte!" I cried. But she didn't reappear.

I should have known she'd be too scared to jump.

Next to me, Patty howled loudly. "I want my sister!"

I knew I had to get Patty out of the tent. Then I could look for Charlotte.

I scooted Patty toward the sidewall of the tent. "Crawl under," I told Patty.

"What about Charlotte?" Patty asked, her voice small, her eyes huge.

"I'll find her," I promised.

I hoped I could keep that promise.

Patty dropped to her belly and wriggled under the sidewall. But the tent wall was taut, and the opening was too tight.

Partway through, Patty stopped and cried, "I'm stuck!"

I pushed at her bottom. She didn't move.

Just then, I heard my name. I whirled to see Will running under the risers toward me. He dodged a flaming piece of canvas and waved his arm. I saw something glint in his hand.

"I have a knife," he gasped as he reached my side. He stabbed the canvas wall and sliced it open. Outside air rushed in, and I took a gulp. The fresh air felt good.

I leaned down and gave Patty a gentle push through the opening. "Wait outside for me. For us," I corrected. "Me and Charlotte."

Patty nodded and scrambled away. At least she would be safe.

But will Charlotte? I worried.

"Hurry," Will said, putting his hand on my back. "You go too."

I shook my head. "I have to find Charlotte."

Will's face was calm, but his brows lowered with worry at my words. "Go," he said. "Find your sister. Fast."

I turned and ran toward the center of the tent, away from my one escape.

The smoke was so blinding I almost couldn't see. The panic inside the tent had risen. So many people were still trying to get out.

Why are there so many people still inside? I wondered. The fire seemed to have started an eternity ago.

But I knew time had slowed down. The fire had only been raging for a couple of minutes.

Where would a six-year-old go? I thought frantically.

Suddenly I remembered something my father had once told me. In times of trouble, people often turn toward the familiar.

I turned and ran toward the southeast bleachers, back to where Charlotte had been sitting. Over and over again, I called her name, my voice thick and hoarse with smoke.

A piece of tent fell from above and sizzled on my sweaty arm. Hot, wet wax—smeared over the canvas to make it waterproof—dropped from the ceiling like rain. More screams erupted as people realized what was happening.

The tent was melting.

I was running out of time. I had to find Charlotte.

When I reached the bleachers, my hopes fell to despair. My sister wasn't there.

I spun in circles, scanning the big top. The smoke clogged my vision, but I would know Charlotte anywhere, just by her silhouette.

I didn't see her.

She must have gotten out, I told myself.

I knew I needed to get out too. I needed to save myself. But I didn't want to give up the search for Charlotte.

I pushed toward the next exit but stopped short. A large wire cage—an animal runway—was blocking the exit. Trainers led the animals through the runways before and after an act.

I could see that the animals had made it through, but the runway hadn't been removed yet. People were climbing on top of the metal cage, pushing their way through the gap between the chute and the top of the entrance.

But there wasn't enough room. People were getting stuck.

"Remove the runway!" a burly, bearded man yelled. A drop of hot wax fell on his face, but he continued to yell.

A few other men were pulling on the runway, but too many people were weighing it down. The runway wouldn't move.

The northeast exit was fully blocked. All around, on all sides of the tent, flames raged. In minutes, the tent would collapse.

CHAPTER EIGHT

The Big Top, Northeast Exit
July 6, 1944
2:45 p.m.

I looked around the tent frantically. Maybe
I could make my way back to the main entrance.
It was all the way on the other side of the big top,
but ...

Maybe Charlotte will be there too, I thought.

After all, that was the way we'd come in earlier.
It was possible my sister would think it was the only
way out.

The smoke was blinding. I stumbled toward
what I thought was the main entrance, but I didn't
even know which way I was going.

It was hot—so hot.

And the smell. The canvas tent was burning. Flesh and hair were burning. I gagged when I tried to breathe.

I put my hand against my face to cover the smell. Then I pushed forward through the smoky darkness.

A whoosh of flames ignited something to my right. I realized it was one of the tent poles that held up a section of the roof.

Moments later, the pole collapsed amidst a din of screams. The canvas top flapped and shuddered as it fell. Burning canvas enveloped people below.

Soon the fire would engulf all the tent poles. When that happened, the burning big top would smother us in flames.

"Charlotte!" I screamed, continuing to run. I couldn't afford to stop.

I could see the main exit now, but it was blocked too. There were so many people still trying to get out.

I called my sister's name again and again helplessly. Then, I heard an answer.

"Help!" moaned a familiar voice.

I stumbled toward the sound and almost fell over the person lying near the grandstands. I dropped to my knees, but it wasn't my sister. It was Mrs. Walker.

"Have you seen Charlotte?" I demanded, tugging on Mrs. Walker's arm.

She just stared at me.

"Stand up!" I yelled. "We need to get you out of here."

A splintering crash sounded behind me. Another pole had fallen.

"Come on, Mrs. Walker!" I shouted, pulling harder on her arm.

"My ankle!" she cried, finally seeming to realize where she was. She glanced around, her gaze filled with horror and confusion. "I fell. I told the girls to keep going. Did they make it out?"

I couldn't answer the question. I knew one of the girls—Patty—had. But I had no idea where the Walker girls—or Charlotte—were.

I pulled Mrs. Walker's arms with all my might. She struggled but couldn't stand.

"Leave me," Mrs. Walker gasped. "You have to get out."

Out of nowhere, a man appeared beside me. He grasped my shoulder.

"Go!" he said. "I'll help her. You just go on. Get yourself to safety."

I let go of Mrs. Walker's arm. The man put his arms around her and pulled her to her feet. I hoped they would make it out alive.

I looked around, trying to get my bearings.

It was nearly impossible in the smoke-filled tent.
I realized I was somehow back near the bleachers
where I'd gotten Patty out.

Maybe Charlotte came back here, I thought,
grasping at anything I could come up with. After
all, it was where she'd last seen us. It was worth a
shot.

I ran around to the back of the grandstands.
Charlotte wasn't there, but Will was. He was
standing next to the opening he'd sliced in the
tent, pushing people out, one by one.

"Will!" I shouted, running to him. "Have you
seen Charlotte?"

He turned to look at me and shook his head,
not saying a word. His eyes widened at something
behind me.

I glanced back too. The center pole was in
flames. My mouth opened into a scream, but no
sound came out.

Will grabbed my arm and pushed me through the slit. I stumbled and landed facedown in the dust.

Behind me, the big top collapsed in a roar of flames.

CHAPTER **NINE**

The whoosh of heat and thick black smoke stunned me. I sat up, dazed. Somehow, I was outside the tent.

Will should have been right behind me. But he wasn't there.

People rushed past me toward the tent, hoping to rescue survivors. But the big top was just a mound of smoldering canvas.

No one under it could have survived.

I got to my feet. The scene around me was like a slow-motion film.

A clown moved past, carrying a bucket of water. His face paint had melted, and what looked like tears fell from his eyes.

A woman screamed for her child.

A child screamed for his mother.

All that remained of the big top was a skeleton. One charred pole was left standing. One grandstand stood blackened and empty. Small fires still snapped and danced. Circus wagons outside the big top smoldered, and a concession tent was still aflame.

The circus crew stepped through the burning ruins, launching water and lifting up the fallen canvas to search for survivors. Their faces were worried, sad, angry—heartbroken.

I knew how they felt. The circus they loved so much—the one I'd been so excited to see—had caused so much horror and pain.

I watched in a daze. Plumes of thick black smoke covered the sun. People were no longer screaming in panic. Now they were crying, huddling, and running. Everyone seemed to be searching for someone.

"Child," a man said, "do you need help finding your mother?"

I looked up and realized the man was talking to me. His face was blackened with soot, and the entire shoulder of his shirt had burned away.

I shook my head slowly. "My mother isn't here" was the only thing I could think of to say.

The man nodded and continued on, but his words had awakened me from my daze. I had to find Patty—and Charlotte.

Please let Charlotte be all right, I repeated in my head.

I waded through the throngs of people toward the midway, searching the face of every child I passed.

Then I saw her.

Patty was sitting on the ground, her head swiveling as she frantically searched the crowd. When she saw me, she leaped to her feet and rushed into my arms. I knelt down and clutched her to me, holding her tight.

"Where's Charlotte?" she said into my ear.

I didn't know how to tell her the truth—I had no idea.

Instead I straightened and grabbed Patty's hand. This time, I'd never let go.

"Let's find her," I said, trying desperately to sound upbeat.

But Patty stood still. She was staring at the ruins of the big top.

I put a hand on her shoulder and turned us both around. I didn't want to see the remains of the tent either.

I couldn't stop thinking about the people who'd been trapped underneath when it collapsed.

Is Will among them? I wondered silently.

Is Charlotte?

I knelt next to Patty, thinking about the "twin sense" my mother claimed they shared. I'd never really believed it, but I wanted to now.

"Which way would Charlotte go?" I asked.

Patty just shrugged.

"What does your sense tell you?" I prodded.

"Nothing," she said softly. "I can't hear her anymore."

Hartford Circus Grounds
July 6, 1944
2:55 p.m.

We moved through the crowd toward Barbour Street. In the distance, sirens wailed. All around us, people were rushing to safety. One woman's blouse was burned across her shoulders. Another young woman had burns up her arms. One man carried a crying child.

Many people had escaped, but I knew everyone would remember what had happened. It would be impossible to forget.

Along Barbour Street, elephant trainers were lining up their elephants. The elephants trumpeted. Their noise sent people running in the other direction.

A fire truck pulled up. Firefighters jumped out, pulling a long hose from the truck.

"Stand back!" one firefighter yelled.

The crowd moved aside as the firefighters drew the hose toward the fires near the big top.

Patty watched them, entranced. For a moment, it seemed as if she'd forgotten the horror we'd just been through.

But I hadn't. I probably never would.

I didn't want to go back toward the big top and the scene of the fire. But I knew we had to. We still needed to find Charlotte.

I thought about my father off at war. For three years he'd been on the battlefields. Every day he saw horrible scenes. He treated the wounded and helped the dying.

He was brave, and today more than ever, I needed to be too.

I took one last look up and down Barbour Street—no sign of Charlotte. Cars were backed up along the street. Some were trying to leave. Others were arriving at the grounds to look for loved ones.

Then I saw a familiar-looking woman jump out of the passenger side of a blue coupe. She looked around frantically.

"Mom!" I yelled. Patty and I both stumbled toward her.

Mom gathered us in her arms. "I was so worried!" she exclaimed. "I heard on the radio at work—"

Then she stiffened and stood up straight, looking beyond my shoulder. I knew what she was about to ask.

"Where's Charlotte? Why isn't she with you?" my mother demanded.

Patty and I were both silent for a moment. I didn't know how to begin. My mother had trusted me with the twins. She had told me to stay with them, keep them safe.

And I hadn't.

"It's my fault!" Patty cried suddenly, tears streaming down her face. "I wanted to sit with the Walkers!"

A sob bubbled up in my chest too. I swallowed hard. "I thought they'd be okay with Mrs. Walker—" I began.

I couldn't read my mother's expression. She was staring at me, shaking her head slowly, her mouth carved in stone.

"I jumped!" Patty said through her tears. "But Charlotte was too scared. . . . I didn't want to go without her . . . but she wouldn't . . ."

"We can talk about it later," my mother interrupted. "Where did you last see her?"

I pointed to the big top. "Section J of the grandstands," I said. "Will Murphy helped us escape."

The sob in my chest tightened when I said Will's name.

We began walking toward the big top. Firefighters and police officers surrounded the area now, ordering people to stay back.

What if they wouldn't let us in? We couldn't leave without Charlotte. I wouldn't allow it.

Then I heard my name. "Audrey!"

I looked over to see Vivian running toward us. Her hair was still in place. There didn't seem to be a scratch on her.

I turned away. I did not want to talk to Vivian—not now.

"Audrey!" Vivian gasped again as she reached us. "I saw Charlotte!"

CHAPTER TEN

"Where?" my mother exclaimed, grasping Vivian's shoulder. "Where did you see her?"

Her eyes wide, Vivian looked from my mom to me and then back again. Close up, I saw that her face was red, like she'd been crying. And the sleeve of her blouse was ripped.

Maybe she didn't make it out untouched after all, I realized.

Vivian rubbed the side of her jaw, where a purple bruise was starting to bloom. "She was being carried out on a stretcher," she said.

Her gaze strayed toward Patty, who was listening eagerly. "I mean, I think it was her," she added. "She had one yellow ribbon still in her hair."

Vivian hesitated again.

"Was she hurt?" my mother gasped desperately. "Was she . . . ?"

We all looked toward Patty. *Alive*, my mother was going to say.

Vivian understood the question without it being asked. "Her eyes were closed, but her face wasn't covered," she said.

For the first time since the fire broke out, I felt like I could breathe again. If Vivian was right, Charlotte was still alive. But how badly was she hurt?

My mother turned and ran up to a police officer. He was guiding people away from the destruction.

"Sir," she said, "which hospital are they taking the injured to?"

The officer cleared his throat. "Most are being taken to Municipal Hospital," he told her.

The man glanced over and saw we were listening. He lowered his voice, but I could still hear him.

"The ones who didn't make it are being taken to the State Armory . . . to be identified," he added quietly.

My mother's eyes glistened with tears, but she swallowed hard and thanked him. Then she returned to us.

"We have to find a way to get to the hospital," my mother said. "Vivian, where's your family? Are they all right?"

"Yes," Vivian said, pointing into the distance. "My mom is right over there. Maybe she could drive you to the hospital?"

I was barely listening. I stared down the midway toward the big top. Smoke still wafted in the air.

The crowd had thinned, and I could see that the grandstands, once the only thing standing, had now burned.

Vivian nudged me. "Audrey, come on. Didn't you hear? My mom is taking you to Municipal Hospital to find Charlotte."

As we walked toward Vivian's car, I took one long look back at the circus grounds. Just a few hours earlier, I'd been so happy and full of hope. All I'd wanted was to see the Flying Wallendas.

Now that hope seemed silly. It was nothing compared to the hope that my sister was alive.

In the car, no one spoke except Ellen Lang, Vivian's mother. She patted my mother's arm as she drove and talked about the new trees that had been planted in our neighborhood and the butterflies that visited her garden.

Her words seemed like small talk, but I knew she was trying to take my mother's mind off the worry. Mrs. Lang had lost her own husband in the war, after all. She knew what grief was like.

Patty sat between Vivian and me in the back seat. Her eyes were pinned on the window, as if she were trying to see Charlotte somewhere on the sidewalks as we passed.

Vivian turned to me. "Are you all right?" she asked. She pointed at my arm. "You're burned."

I looked down at my arm. A long burn was blistering on my skin. I hadn't even felt the pain. Now I realized it was stinging.

It was a scar I would wear forever—along with the ones I would carry inside.

"Will Murphy," I said suddenly. "I know he was your friend too."

Vivian stiffened and bit her lip. "Is he okay?" she asked.

I gave a small shake of my head. "He was helping people out of the tent. Right until the very end."

Hartford, Connecticut
Municipal Hospital
July 6, 1944
3:30 p.m.

Municipal Hospital was swarming with people. My mother pushed her way through the crowd to the front desk. Patty and I followed close behind.

"I'm looking for my daughter," she said. "Six years old, brown hair."

The receptionist looked at my mother with tired eyes. "Do you have a photograph?"

My mother reached for her purse as Patty piped up. "She looks just like me! We're twins."

The receptionist managed a smile at Patty, then stood up and told us to follow her.

We waited in a small room for what felt like hours. Finally, a doctor walked in. He looked even more tired than the receptionist. But he also managed to smile at Patty.

"I can't believe it!" he said. "There's two of you! Is your sister's name Charlotte? She's here. She's doing just fine."

All the sobs I'd been holding in erupted. I put my hands to my face, feeling hot tears streaming through my fingers. Charlotte was alive. At last, we'd found her.

The doctor led us to the room Charlotte was in. When we walked in, she sat up and squealed in delight. She looked so tiny on the hospital bed.

My mother hugged Charlotte first, then Patty did the same. Finally, it was my turn. I held Charlotte tight until she squirmed.

"I'm in the hospital!" she told us. "The nurses are really nice. I even got some ice cream!"

Patty crawled into the bed next to her. "Now I'm in the hospital too!" she announced.

As the girls cuddled together, the doctor told us what had happened. Charlotte had been found by the animal runway, near the northeast exit, under a pile of bodies. They thought she must have fallen, and others fell on top of her.

Those bodies had shielded her when the burning canvas fell. She didn't have a single burn on her. Rescuers had heard her whimpering and pulled her free.

I had been there, at the northeast exit. I'd been so close to her.

How could I have missed her? I scolded myself. If I had found her, Charlotte wouldn't have had to go through such horror.

I bit my lip, trying to hold back my tears.

The doctor noticed my stricken face. "She doesn't remember any of it," he said. "The mind sometimes erases severe trauma. She might have some bad dreams, but she'll be okay."

"She's one of the lucky ones," my mother said softly.

My eyes filled with tears again, and I turned back toward the hospital bed, where my sisters sat arm in arm, giggling. My Amazing Adams Twins. We were the lucky ones indeed.

Hartford, Connecticut
Municipal Hospital
One month later

I twirled on one toe and dropped into a curtsy. Next to me, Vivian did a little tap dance and curtsied too.

The little girl in the hospital bed clapped loudly. "Bravo!" she said.

I reached into our bag of goodies and pulled out a small stuffed bear. The little girl squealed as I handed it to her. She hugged it tight.

Vivian and I smiled at each other. For the past two weeks, we'd been giving daily performances to kids in the hospital. Vivian had taught me some tap dance moves, and we both sang and danced for the kids.

It had been Vivian's idea. We'd both attended Will Murphy's funeral a few days after the fire. It had been packed with kids from school, teachers, and parents. Even the mayor of Hartford was there. Everyone talked about what a hero Will was. He'd saved so many, helping others without thinking of himself.

After the funeral, Vivian had approached me on my way out of the church. She'd breathlessly told me about her idea.

"We could do a little song-and-dance routine at the hospital," she'd said. "And maybe give the kids some gifts. It would make their day better!"

"I don't know," I'd said.

Since the fire, I hadn't even thought about performing. My dream of becoming an aerialist was over. I wasn't sure I ever wanted to go to a circus again.

Vivian had been persistent. "The twins can join us too," she'd offered.

"No," I'd said, shaking my head. "The twins don't want to perform anymore. They just want to play with the Walker girls."

The Walker girls had made it out of the big top. Mrs. Walker, amazingly, had made it out as well— thanks to the nice man. Her ankle was broken and she had some burns, but otherwise she was fine.

Charlotte was fine too—physically—and had been released from the hospital right away. Mentally, she was still healing.

We all were. Every night my mother gathered us around and had us talk about the fire—our fears, our sadness, our regrets. It felt good to cry and let it out.

I'd turned Vivian down that day, but the following week, a letter from my father had arrived.

He'd written to me as soon as he'd heard about the fire on the army radio.

Take some time to be sad, he'd said. *But don't let anything keep you from becoming what you want to be.*

Reading his letter had forced me think about Vivian's idea. I thought about all the heroes from that day. The man who'd helped Mrs. Walker. Will Murphy, who'd died helping others.

I wasn't a hero, not exactly. But now I saw my chance to help.

A few days later, I'd gone to Vivian's house. "I'll do it," I'd told her with a smile.

Vivian had squealed and hugged me, and I'd hugged her back.

At first, we'd performed for the kids who had been burned or injured in the circus fire. Then we'd started performing for all children in the hospital, no matter what they were there for.

Many of the kids we performed for had severe burns. Some had broken limbs. But all were happy to see us. Our performances gave them a reason to laugh.

Now, Vivian hugged me again. We waved goodbye to the little girl and walked down the hall to the next room.

Vivian linked her arm through mine and gave a little skip. I laughed. We weren't exactly friends, not yet. But together, we were survivors.

A NOTE FROM THE AUTHOR

The Hartford Circus Fire was a terrible tragedy. The fire broke out just minutes after the afternoon performance began on July 6, 1944. Between 6,000 and 8,000 people were inside the big top that day. The fire killed at least 167 people, mostly women and children. More than 700 were injured. None of the circus animals were killed.

In 1944, the Ringling Bros. and Barnum & Bailey Circus was the largest circus in the United States. The circus traveled the country, moving from town to town by train. The main performance was under a tent called the big top, which could seat up to 9,000 spectators.

No one knows exactly how the fire started, only that it began in the southwest corner of the big top, near the men's restroom. One man in attendance told an usher that someone threw a cigarette. Six years later, a man named Robert Segee confessed to setting the fire. During the summer of 1944, he had been a sixteen-year-old roustabout for the circus. He told police he'd had a nightmare that had made him do it. Years later, Segee denied setting the fire. Many investigators and historians don't believe he was the culprit.

The canvas big top tent was coated with gasoline and paraffin wax to make it waterproof. The wax mixture was highly flammable. As the tent went up in flames, melting wax rained down on people below, badly burning them. The melting wax caused more panic, as spectators desperately tried to escape the tent and the falling wax. Many people died from being burned, but many also died from being trampled during the panic. Others died when they were struck by falling tent poles or other structures. And still others died in the pileup at the northeast exit.

When I started researching the book, I was drawn in by the many accounts of survival and heroism. One man named Bill Curlee climbed on top of the animal runway that was blocking the exit. Then he lifted children up and pushed them through to safety. He did this over and over until a nearby support pole fell, killing him. Another story tells of a teenage boy who slit the tent open and helped people through before escaping himself. In my story, this boy became Will Murphy.

Circus workers proved to be heroes as well. Fred Bradna, the ringmaster, helped carry children to safety. Clown Emmett Kelly threw buckets of water on the fire. Ushers helped people exit in an orderly fashion.

Children became separated from their parents in the crush of people. Alone, they figured out ways to survive. One little boy's foot got stuck in the animal runway as he was climbing over. He reached down, untied his shoe, shook it off, and was able to scramble away.

I was also inspired by the survival story of Joan Smith, a twelve-year-old girl. When the fire broke out, she got up to leave. But the seats on the risers below her were crammed with people. She looked behind and saw that the risers above her were empty. She quickly scaled the risers. When she got to the top, she jumped down, bending her knees to avoid injury. With her quick thinking and bravery, she saved herself.

Joan's cleverness made its way into Audrey's story. When I was planning the book, I imagined a young girl who sees an opportunity to escape. My character would brave the heights and help others too. But I wasn't sure yet who she would be. Who would she help? And what would the circus mean to her?

Children and adults of all ages love to attend the circus. People love the death-defying high-wire acts, the music, the animals, the lights. They love the sideshows and the costumes. They love the clowns and the concessions. But what would make my character's love for the circus unique? I imagined a girl whose dream was to become a performer herself. Going to the circus would mean so much to her. And her love for the circus would make the fire much more tragic.

But, despite it all, she learns to love performing again. She perseveres, and she survives. I hope you find inspiration in Audrey's story. Like her, you can follow your dreams. And like Audrey, you can be brave, overcome obstacles that stand in your way, and persevere.

MAKING CONNECTIONS

1. What are some conditions that led to so many deaths under the big top in the Hartford Circus Fire? What could have been done differently to prevent deaths?

2. Audrey often writes letters to her father, who is away at war. Imagine that you are Audrey. Write a letter telling your father about the circus fire. What details would you include? Are there any details you would choose to leave out?

3. Audrey makes a choice to find Charlotte rather than escape the tent. What might have happened if she had made a different choice?

GLOSSARY

aerialist (AIR-ee-uh-list)—a person who performs feats in the air or above the ground, especially on a trapeze

Allied forces (AL-lyd FOR-siz)—countries united against Germany during World War II, including France, the United States, Canada, Great Britain, and others

coupe (koop)—a car that has two doors and room for four, or sometimes only two, people

cue (Q)—a word or action that signals an actor to go on stage

demeanor (di-MEE-ner)—behavior toward others

enlist (en-LIST)—to voluntarily join a branch of the military

finale (fi-NAL-ee)—the last part of something, such as a performance or play

grandstand (GRAND-stand)—a seating structure for viewers at an event

medic (MED-ik)—a soldier trained to give medical help in an emergency or during a battle

menagerie (muh-NAJ-uh-ree)—a place where animals are kept and trained

midway (MID-wey)—an avenue at a carnival or circus for food stands, games, and side exhibits

occupation (awk-yuh-PAY-shuhn)—taking over and controlling another country with an army

pygmy (PIG-mee)—smaller than the usual size

roustabout (ROUST-uh-bout)—a circus worker who puts up and takes down tents, cares for the grounds, and handles animals or equipment

sideshow (SAHYD-shoh)—a small show off to the side offered in addition to the main show

silhouette (sil-oo-ET)—an outline of something that shows its shape

spectator (SPEK-tay-tur)—a person who watches an event

superstition (soo-pur-STI-shuhn)—a belief that an action can affect the outcome of a future event

trapeze (tra-PEEZ)—a short, horizontal bar hung from two parallel ropes and used by acrobats

trauma (TRAW-muh)—a very difficult or unpleasant experience that causes someone to have mental or emotional problems, usually for a long time

villa (VIL-uh)—a large fancy house especially one in the country

ABOUT THE AUTHOR

photo credit: Anda Marie Photography

Jessica Gunderson grew up in the small town of Washburn, North Dakota. She has a bachelor's degree from the University of North Dakota and an MFA in creative writing from Minnesota State University, Mankato. She has written more than seventy-five books for young readers. Her book *President Lincoln's Killer and the America He Left Behind* won a 2018 Eureka! Nonfiction Children's Book Silver Award. Jessica currently lives in Madison, Wisconsin, with her husband and three cats.

ABOUT THE ILLUSTRATOR

photo credit: Wendy Tan

Wendy Tan is a Chinese-Malaysian illustrator based in Kuala Lumpur, Malaysia. Over the past few years, she has contributed to numerous animation productions and advertisements. Now Wendy's passion for storytelling has led her down a new path: children's book illustration. When she's not drawing, Wendy likes to spend time playing with her mix-breed rescue dog, Lucky.